First published 2021 by Walker Books Ltd, 87 Vauxhall Walk, London SE11 5HJ   Text © 2021 Joyce Dunbar
Illustrations © 2021 Petr Horáček   The right of Joyce Dunbar and Petr Horáček to be identified as author and illustrator
respectively of this work has been asserted by them in accordance with the Copyright, Designs and Patents Act 1988

2 4 6 8 10 9 7 5 3 1

This book has been typeset in Avenir   Printed in China   All rights reserved. No part of this book may be reproduced, transmitted
or stored in an information retrieval system in any form or by any means, graphic, electronic or mechanical, including photocopying,
taping and recording, without prior written permission from the publisher.   British Library Cataloguing in Publication Data: a catalogue
record for this book is available from the British Library   ISBN 978-1-4063-9568-6   www.walker.co.uk

WALKER BOOKS
AND SUBSIDIARIES
LONDON · BOSTON · SYDNEY · AUCKLAND

To my cat, Minnie
HaHa – J.D.

To my sister Markéta,
with love – P.H.

JOYCE DUNBAR ILLUSTRATED BY PETR HORÁČEK

MISTER BOO!

There was once a cat called Mister Boo.

Why was he called Mister Boo?

Because when he first arrived at his new home

with Rosie, he poked his head out of the box

so suddenly that he made her jump.

"How do you do, Mister Boo!" she laughed.

It was a lot of fun.

Mister Boo liked fun. Again …
and again … and again.

He crept up very silently on anything
that moved…
He pricked up his bat-cat ears and
swished his tail. He crouched and
stretched his neck until his face
loomed very close.
His green eyes glittered,
his nose twitched,
his whiskers bristled.

Then he pounced ...

BOO!

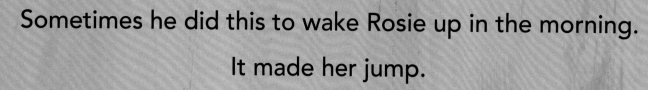

Sometimes he did this to wake Rosie up in the morning.

It made her jump.

"SHOO, MISTER BOO!"

she scolded.

Once he climbed into the goldfish bowl because he wanted to play with the fishes.

"SHOO, MISTER BOO!"

said Rosie, flipping the goldfish back into their bowl.

Mister Boo was happy all year round.

He liked the summer when the sun made the grass

shine and dandelions sprouted everywhere.

He liked the autumn when the
leaves danced and twirled.

He liked the winter with the snow and the warm fires and laps to sit on.

But best of all, he liked the SPRING!

In spring there was such a fluttering and flouncing, such a twitching and stirring. Everything **MOVED**.

And Mister Boo, I'm sorry to say, got up to all sorts of mischief.

He frightened the baby birds
when they were learning to fly.

He scattered the baby rabbits when they were taking their first look at the world.

He shocked the baby owls from their treetops,

so that the poor mother owl had to rescue them.

He was **WICKED!**

But he wasn't wicked on purpose. He was just adding to the

gaiety of spring, joining in with the fun and frolics.

Time passed, until one winter came, with dark mornings and early nights. Mister Boo slept for longer and longer, more than he ever had before.

He was finally woken by the twittering of birdsong and the smell of fresh air. Oh dear! He had overslept and spring was in full swing without him.

When he tried to spring into action, he felt achy and stiff. He could hardly squeeze through his cat-flap.

He peered into a squirrel hole and tried to say BOO to a baby squirrel. But his eyes were no longer so glittery and not at all scary. The squirrel stared back and skipped right over him.

He clawed his way to a treetop and tried to say BOO to a chaffinch. But his ears were no longer so pointy and fierce.

"Have a nice day," it chirruped.

He tried to say BOO to a diadem spider.

But he was so slow and clumsy.

"Mind my web!" said the spider.

"It's delicate."

And when he tried to say BOO to a mother owl,

she pecked him, right on the nose!

OUCH!

What has happened to me? pondered Mister Boo.
I seem to have lost some of my pounce. I'm not
so much fun any more.

He sloped sadly off home and crept
in through his cat-flap.

"Mister Boo!" Rosie cried. "Where have you been?

I've been looking everywhere for you."

She scooped him up in her arms and gave

him his favourite meal of sardines.

When he had eaten them and licked himself clean,

she said, "Look! I've got a surprise for you."

Next to his basket was another, smaller basket.

Inside was a ball of yellow fur.

What is it? wondered Mister Boo, giving it a sniff.

The little yellow ball uncurled
and sprang to greet him.
It was a kitten!

"Meet Dandelion," said Rosie.
And the little yellow kitten went ...